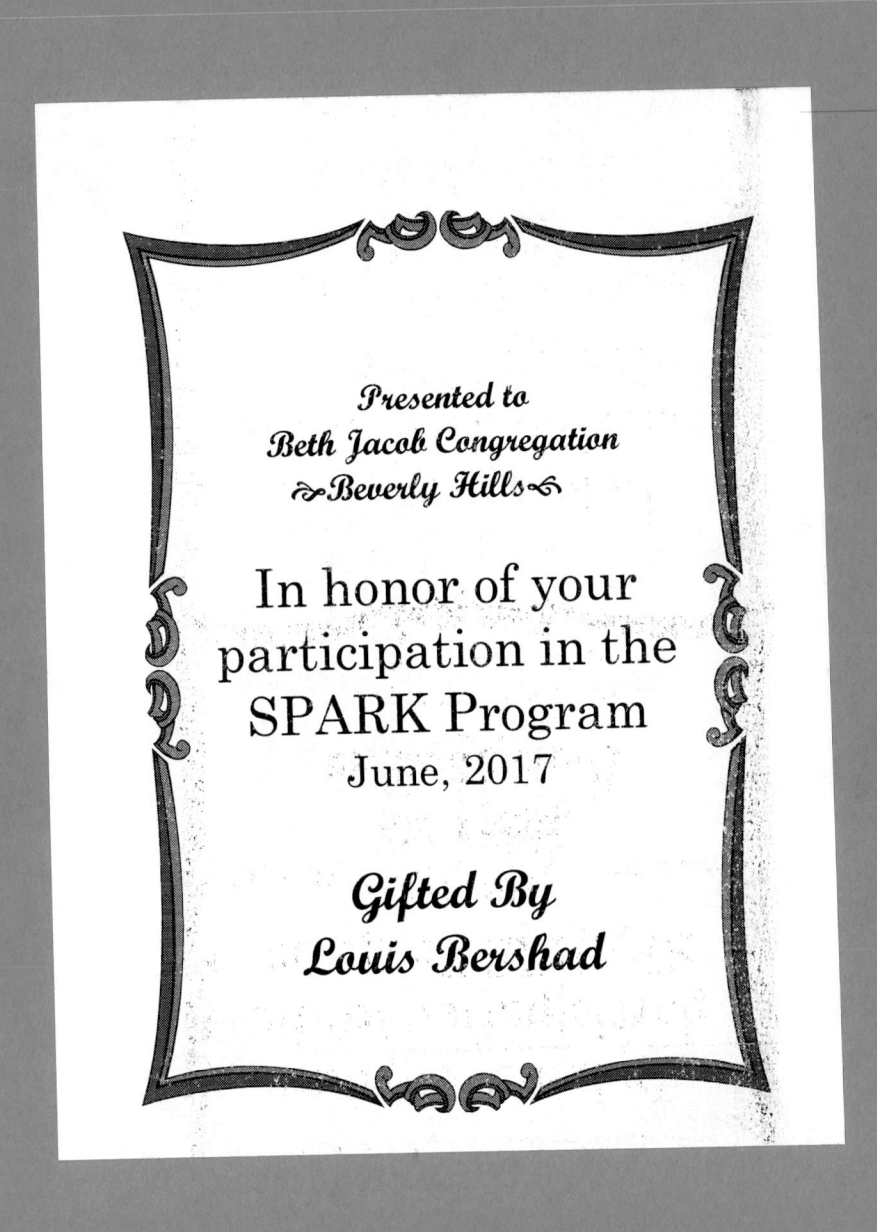

Presented to
Beth Jacob Congregation
Beverly Hills

In honor of your
participation in the
SPARK Program
June, 2017

Gifted By
Louis Bershad

מסורה

ArtScroll Youth Series

Rabbi Nosson Scherman / Rabbi Meir Zlotowitz
General Editors

THE GRAFF-RAND EDITION

ספר הברכות שלי

Published by
Mesorah Publications, ltd

ArtScroll Children's Book of Berachos

by Shmuel Blitz

Illustrated by Tova Katz

Introduction by
Rabbi Nosson Scherman

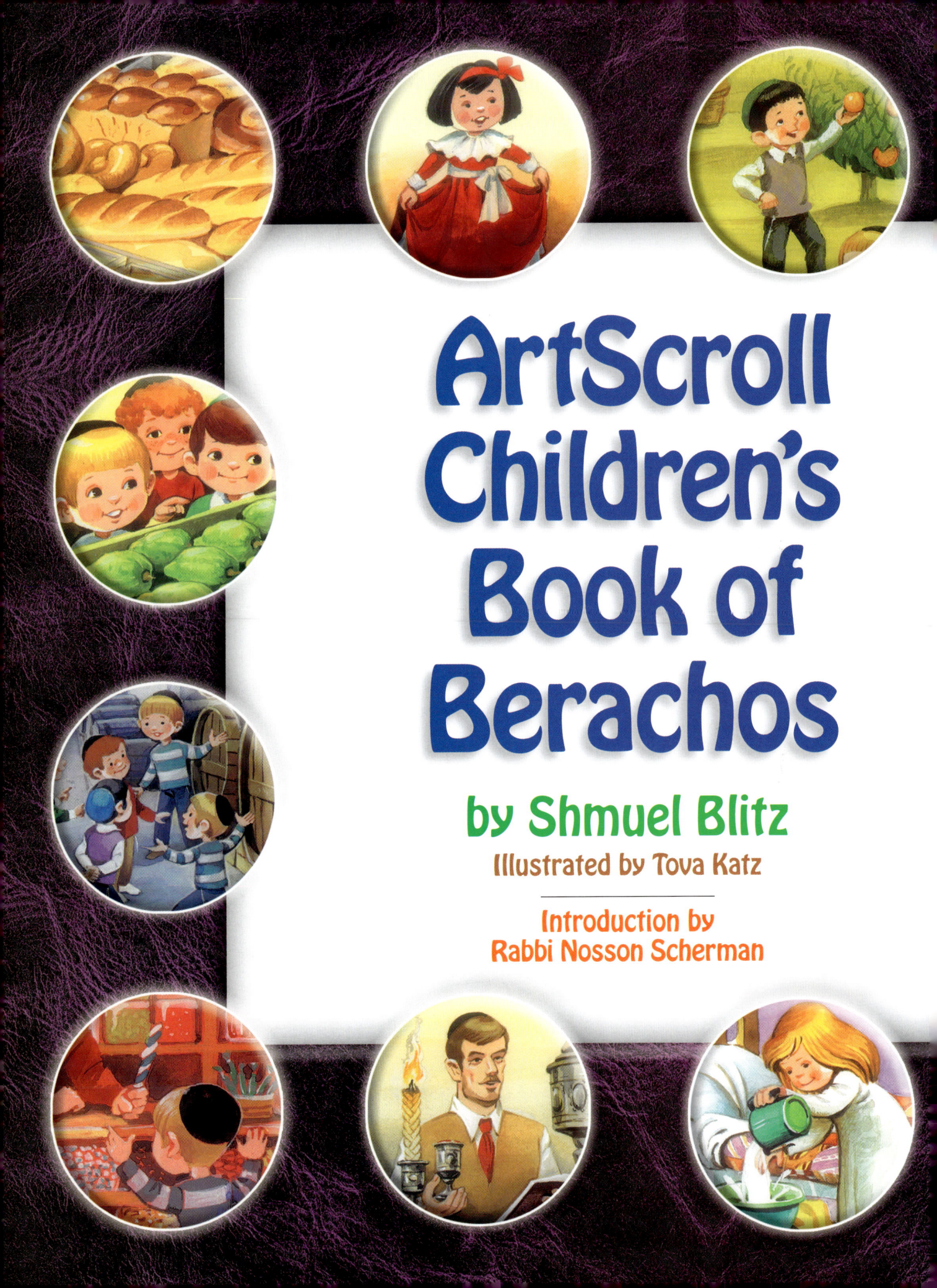

This volume is dedicated in loving memory of our parents

ר' מאיר חיים ב"ר יקותיאל ז"ל
נפטר ד' תשרי תשד"מ

פריידא ריקלא בת הרב משה נתן ע"ה
נפטרה כ"ז אייר תשמ"ו

למשפחת גראף

Meyer H. and Joy Ruth (Taxon) Graff ז"ל

ר' חיים ב"ר יוסף משה ז"ל
נפטר כ"ח תשרי תשס"ג

ראניא בת ישראל ע"ה
נפטרה י"ט שבט תשנ"ט

למשפחת ראנד

Chaim and Ronia (Grinfogel) Rand ז"ל

and grandparents זכרונם לברכה

who overcame many challenges to create a family dedicated to faith in Hashem and loyalty to Torah and mitzvos. Baruch Hashem, they persevered and succeeded. Our primary goal has been to carry on their legacy by raising future generations in their image. It is in their *zchus* that we have been able to raise children who are *bnei* and *bnos Torah* and who are raising their own new generation of *bnei* and *bnos Torah*.

The theme of *Berachos/Blessings* is gratitude and continuity, because, as the commentators explain, the word *berachah* refers to Hashem as a continuous wellspring of blessing. In an age and culture when faith in Hashem and allegiance to Torah are under constant siege, acknowledgment of His constant presence in our lives and gratitude for His gifts are the foundation of any efforts to convey the legacy of our forebears to the next generation.

It is fitting, therefore, that we honor the memory of our parents and grandparents with this volume, for it imbues young children with the meaning and laws of *berachos* and thereby inspires them with gratitude to the Giver of all blessings and the privilege of thanking Him for every joy and pleasure in life.

Jacob M.M. and Pnina (Rand) Graff

Malka Ita and Boruch Blum – Meir   Ronia Rochel   Tzipora   Devora

Chaya Rivka Graff

Meira Chava and Elie Portnoy – Chaim   Zev

Joy and Adam Kushnir – Yehoshua Meir   Tziporah

Meir Reuven Yekusiel and Itta Graff

Ahuva Esther Graff

FIRST EDITION *First Impression* … November 2011

ARTSCROLL SERIES® / ARTSCROLL CHILDREN'S BOOK OF BERACHOS — THE GRAFF-RAND EDITION

© Copyright 2011, by MESORAH PUBLICATIONS, Ltd., 4401 Second Avenue / Brooklyn, NY 11232 / (718) 921-9000 / www.artscroll.com

ALL RIGHTS RESERVED. The text, prefatory and associated textual contents and introductions have been designed, edited and revised as to content, form and style. **No part of this book may be reproduced IN ANY FORM, PHOTOCOPYING, OR COMPUTER RETRIEVAL SYSTEMS** — even for personal use without written permission from the copyright holder. **THE RIGHTS OF THE COPYRIGHT HOLDER WILL BE STRICTLY ENFORCED.**

ISBN 10: 1-4226-1170-1 / ISBN 13: 978-1-4226-1170-8

Typography by CompuScribe at ArtScroll Studios, Ltd.

Printed in the United States of America by Noble Book Press Corp.   •   Bound by Sefercraft, Quality Bookbinders, Ltd., Brooklyn N.Y. 11232

Table of Contents

6 Introduction

Section 1
בִּרְכַּת הַנֶּהֱנִין   Bircas HaNehenin

הַמּוֹצִיא	8	HaMotzi
מְזוֹנוֹת	9	Mezonos
הַגֶּפֶן	10	HaGafen
הָעֵץ	11	HaEitz
הָאֲדָמָה	12	HaAdamah
שֶׁהַכֹּל	13	Shehakol
בְּשָׂמִים	14	Besamim
בִּרְכַּת הַמָּזוֹן	15-26	Bircas HaMazon
בּוֹרֵא נְפָשׁוֹת	27	Borei Nefashos
עַל הַמִּחְיָה - בִּרְכַּת מֵעֵין שָׁלֹשׁ	28	Al HaMichyah – Bircas Me'ein Shalosh
שִׁבְעַת הַמִּינִים	30	Shivas HaMinim

Section 2
בִּרְכַּת הַמִּצְוֹת   Bircas HaMitzvos

נְטִילַת יָדַיִם	32	Netilas Yadayim
בִּרְכַּת הַתּוֹרָה	33	Bircas HaTorah
צִיצִת	34	Tzitzis
מְזוּזָה	35	Mezuzah
נְטִילַת לוּלָב	36	Lulav
הַדְלָקַת נֵרוֹת	37	Candle Lighting
נֵרוֹת חֲנֻכָּה	38	Chanukah Candles

Section 3
בִּרְכַּת הַהוֹדָאָה וְהַשֶּׁבַח   Bircas HaHoda'ah V'HaShevach

אֲשֶׁר יָצַר	40	Asher Yatzar
שֶׁהֶחֱיָנוּ	41	Shehecheyanu
בָּרָק - רַעַם	42-43	Lightning – Thunder
קֶשֶׁת	44	Rainbow
יָם	45	Ocean
בִּרְכַּת הָאִילָנוֹת	46	Fruit Tree Blooming
בְּשׂוֹרוֹת טוֹבוֹת - בְּשׂוֹרוֹת רָעוֹת	47	Good News – Bad News
חַכְמֵי יִשְׂרָאֵל	48	Torah Scholar

Introduction
Why do we need to say berachos?

Thank You, Hashem

Just imagine that you are in jail. You are kept in a room with no light and no window. Your hands and feet are chained, so you can hardly move. It is hard for you to sleep, so you are always tired. You are given very little to eat, so you are always hungry.

Then, one day, someone opens the door of your cell. A man with a big smile on his face says, "You are free!" The man takes off your chains and gives you a delicious meal. He gently helps you stand up and walks you outside to see the sunshine and breathe fresh air.

He puts money into your pocket and takes you home. He tells you that whenever you need something, you can always call him. He is your friend and he will always help you.

What will you say? You will say, "How can I thank you! I love you! You are my best friend! I don't know how to thank you enough! I don't know the right words to say it!"

Our best friend is Hashem. He gives us health, the bright sun, healthy food, the ability to walk, see, sing, hear, learn, and grow. How can we thank Him? We thank Him by saying a *berachah* whenever we enjoy His world or do a mitzvah.

When we say a *berachah*, we show Hashem that we know everything we have comes from Him, and we thank Him for it.

The Talmud wonders about two verses that seem to say different things. One verse says that everything belongs to Hashem. The other verse says that He gave the world to us. The Talmud explains that before we say a *berachah*, everything is Hashem's, but when we thank Him with a *berachah*, He gives it to us. Hashem wants us to enjoy His world, but it is also important for us to know that it is Hashem Who made us and gives us everything we need. He is kind and always wants to give to us. We have to try hard to deserve it.

This wonderful book shows us many, many of the gifts that Hashem gives us and teaches us what *berachos* to say. We are grateful to Shmuel Blitz for writing it, and to Tova Katz for illustrating it. And we are grateful to Hashem for the beautiful world He gave us and for teaching us how He wants us to live.

Marcheshvan 5772 / November 2011   **Rabbi Nosson Scherman**

The author dedicates this book to his newest granddaughter,
Maya Ayelet Schlesinger

Section 1

בִּרְכַּת הַנֶּהֱנִין
Bircas HaNehenin

Berachos on food and other things you eat, drink, and enjoy.

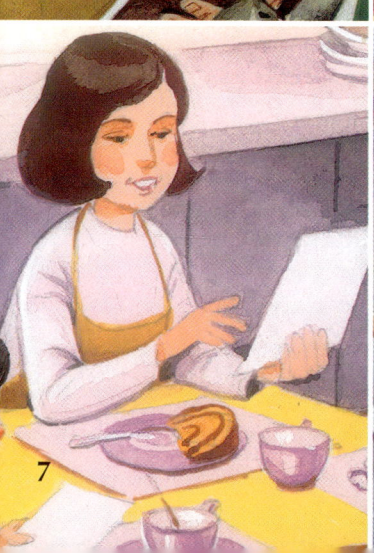

HaMotzi / הַמּוֹצִיא

When you wash your hands before you eat bread, you say:

בָּרוּךְ אַתָּה יהוה אֱלֹהֵינוּ מֶלֶךְ הָעוֹלָם, אֲשֶׁר קִדְּשָׁנוּ בְּמִצְוֹתָיו, וְצִוָּנוּ עַל נְטִילַת יָדָיִם.

Blessed are You, Hashem, our God, King of the universe, Who has made us holy with His mitzvos, and commanded us about washing our hands.

Before you eat bread, you say:

בָּרוּךְ אַתָּה יְיָ, אֱלֹהֵינוּ מֶלֶךְ הָעוֹלָם, הַמּוֹצִיא לֶחֶם מִן הָאָרֶץ.

Blessed are You, Hashem, our God, King of the universe, Who brings out bread from the ground.

A Closer Look

Saying *HaMotzi* on bread is so important that after you make *HaMotzi*, you do not have to make the usual *berachos* on most other foods you will eat during that meal.

Some foods are more important than others. Bread is the most important food. That is why *HaMotzi* refers to one specific food — bread. If you plan to eat many foods, the first *berachah* to say is *HaMotzi*.

Some *HaMotzi* Foods: bagel, bread, challah, English muffin, matzoh, rolls

Did You Know??

The *berachah* of *HaMotzi* has ten words in it. It is interesting that there are also ten words in the *pasuk* in *Tehillim* 104:14: מַצְמִיחַ חָצִיר לַבְּהֵמָה, וְעֵשֶׂב לַעֲבֹדַת הָאָדָם; לְהוֹצִיא לֶחֶם מִן הָאָרֶץ. — Hashem causes grass to grow for the animals, and plants to grow through man's work, and brings out bread from the ground.

8

Mezonos / מְזוֹנוֹת

Before eating products made from five kinds of grain: wheat, barley, rye, oats, or spelt (for example, cake, cookies, pretzels, spaghetti, and noodles), you say:

Blessed are You, Hashem, our God, King of the universe, Who creates different kinds of nourishment.

בָּרוּךְ אַתָּה יְיָ, אֱלֹהֵינוּ מֶלֶךְ הָעוֹלָם, בּוֹרֵא מִינֵי מְזוֹנוֹת.

A Closer Look
In order for any type of grain to grow, a seed must be planted in the ground. After that we trust Hashem to take care of it by making sure there is plenty of sun and rain. Then a farmer works every day, to make sure the crop is watered and stays healthy, while it grows and becomes a food we can eat. It is the same with you. After you are born, we count on Hashem to make sure all is well, and your parents watch over you and make sure you grow up healthy and wise.

Did You Know??
Every *berachah* must include the words "*Melech HaOlam*," which says that Hashem is King of the universe.

If you will eat different kinds of food in front of you, you say the *berachah* of *Mezonos* before the *berachos* for wine, fruits, and vegetables.

Some *Mezonos* Foods: barley (cooked), blintzes, bran muffins, brownies, cake, casseroles, cinnamon rolls, cookies, couscous, cream puffs, danishes, doughnuts, farina, hamantashen, knishes, macaroni, muffins, noodle pudding, oatmeal, pancakes, pastries, pies, pizza, pretzels, rice, rice cakes, rice kugel, spaghetti, wafers

HaGafen / הַגֶּפֶן

Before drinking wine or grape juice, you say:

Blessed are You, Hashem, our God, King of the universe, Who creates the fruit of the grapevine.

בָּרוּךְ אַתָּה יְיָ, אֱלֹהֵינוּ מֶלֶךְ הָעוֹלָם, בּוֹרֵא פְּרִי הַגָּפֶן.

A Closer Look

King David wrote in *Tehillim*, "Wine makes a person's heart happy" (104:15). It is a very special drink that can make a man glad when he drinks it in small amounts, but if he drinks too much, it can make him sick.

The first thing Noach did after the Flood was plant grapes so he could drink wine. He became drunk and was embarrassed. He should not have planted grapes first, before planting anything else.

Did You Know??

Wine (and grape juice) is considered a special drink. It is the only liquid that has its very own blessing. We use wine at many important events in our lives. We use wine at a wedding, at a *bris*, on Shabbos, on Yom Tov — and of course on Pesach, when we drink four cups of wine at the Seder. We also use wine when we say *Havdalah* at the end of Shabbos and Yom Tov.

Why do we use wine at so many of these events? We learn in *Sefer Shoftim* (9:13), "The grapevine said, 'Shall I give away my wine that makes Hashem and man happy?'" This teaches us that not only does wine make man happy, but it also, in some way, makes Hashem "happy." That is why the *Kohanim* poured wine on the Altar when offerings were brought in the *Beis HaMikdash* and why we use wine at so many events.

How long has man been drinking wine? Some Rabbis say that the fruit that Adam and Eve ate in the Garden of Eden was really a grape that Adam had turned into wine.

Some *HaGafen* Foods: grape juice, wine

HaEitz / הָעֵץ

Before eating fruit that grows on trees that produce fruit year after year (for example, olives, apples, pears, and oranges), you say:

בָּרוּךְ אַתָּה יְיָ, אֱלֹהֵינוּ מֶלֶךְ הָעוֹלָם, בּוֹרֵא פְּרִי הָעֵץ.

Blessed are You, Hashem, our God, King of the universe, Who creates the fruit of the tree.

Did You Know??
There are four Jewish New Years. Tu B'Shvat (the 15th day of the month of Shvat) is the New Year for trees. There is a custom to eat many different fruits on Tu B'Shvat. We try to include fruits from Eretz Yisrael.

A Closer Look
Before we make a *berachah*, the food belongs to Hashem and we are not allowed to eat it. After we make the *berachah*, Hashem says that the food belongs to us.

Did You Know??
We say "*Borei Pri HaEitz*" only on trees that grow fruit year after year. We don't say a "*Borei Pri HaEitz*" on the fruit of trees that have to be planted every year, such as bananas, or on the fruit that grow on most bushes, such as pineapples, but say *Borei Pri HaAdamah* instead.

When you have different kinds of food in front of you, you say the *berachah* of HaEitz before the *berachah* of HaAdamah.

Some *HaEitz* Foods: almonds, apples, apricots, avocados, cashews, cherries, coconuts, dates, grapes, grapefruits, nectarines, olives, oranges, peaches, pears, pistachio nuts, plums, tangerines, walnuts

HaAdamah / הָאֲדָמָה

Before eating other foods that grow from the ground,
(such as watermelon, bananas, tomatoes, lettuce, and cucumber), you say:

Blessed are You, Hashem, our God, King of the universe, Who creates the fruit of the ground.

בָּרוּךְ אַתָּה יהוה אֱלֹהֵינוּ מֶלֶךְ הָעוֹלָם,
בּוֹרֵא פְּרִי הָאֲדָמָה

A Closer Look

When you make a *berachah*, you are showing that you know that Hashem created the world and runs every detail of the world, every minute of the day. Hashem watches over everything that happens; otherwise, nothing would grow.

Did You Know??

If you learned the laws but are not sure which *berachah* to make on a certain fruit, and there is no one around to ask, you should say "*Borei Pri HaAdamah*," because all trees grow from the ground.

If you will eat different kinds of food in front of you, you say the *berachah* of *HaAdamah* before the *berachah* of *Shehakol*.

Some *HaAdamah* Foods: arbes (chickpeas), baked beans, bananas, beets, cabbage, canteloupes, carrots, celery, corn, cucumbers, eggplant, green beans, kasha, lettuce, lima beans, peanuts, peas, pickles, pineapple, potatoes, squash, strawberries, sunflower seeds, tomatoes, watermelon, zucchini

Shehakol / שֶׁהַכֹּל

Before eating or drinking foods such as meat, fish, eggs, ice cream, soda, and candy, you say:

בָּרוּךְ אַתָּה יהוה אֱלֹהֵינוּ מֶלֶךְ הָעוֹלָם, שֶׁהַכֹּל נִהְיֶה בִּדְבָרוֹ.

Blessed are You, Hashem, our God, King of the universe, through Whose word everything is created.

A Closer Look
You are allowed to say a *berachah* in the language that you understand. But it is best to say a *berachah* in Hebrew.

Did You Know??
If you learned the laws and are still not sure which *berachah* to recite on a certain food, and there is no one there to ask, you should say *Shehakol*, which includes "everything that is created."

Some *Shehakol* Foods: candy, cheese, chicken, chocolate, eggs, fish, fruit juice, ice cream, ices, meat, milk, soda, water

Besamim / בְּשָׂמִים

When you smell nice fragrances from different spices, you say:

Blessed are You, Hashem, our God, King of the universe, Who creates all the different types of spices and smells.

בָּרוּךְ אַתָּה יהוה אֱלֹהֵינוּ מֶלֶךְ הָעוֹלָם, בּוֹרֵא מִינֵי בְשָׂמִים.

A Closer Look

You have five different senses — taste, smell, sight, touch, and hearing. Among these five senses, smell is considered the most spiritual. In fact, the Gemara teaches us that the pleasures of smell are felt directly by a person's *neshamah* (soul).

Some say that this is because when Adam and Chavah were in the Garden of Eden, they *tasted* the fruit, they *saw* the fruit, they *touched* the fruit, Chavah *heard* the snake who made her sin, and Adam *heard* Chavah who made him sin. They sinned with those four senses, but they did not sin by smelling.

When Shabbos is over, and we make *Havdalah*, we say a *berachah* on fragrant spices. *Havdalah* uses all five of our senses: *Tasting* the wine, *smelling* the spices, *looking* at the flame, *feeling* its heat, and *hearing* the *berachos* that are being said.

One reason for the spices is to make us happier, because we are sad that Shabbos is coming to an end and the extra *neshamah* that we have on Shabbos is going away. When *Havdalah* is finished, we say to each other, "Have a good week." Some people even begin dancing to celebrate the new week.

Did You Know??

Berachos remind us that the purpose of our lives is to make ourselves holy.

Grace After Meals / בִּרְכַּת הַמָּזוֹן

On Shabbos and holidays, we recite the following psalm before Bircas HaMazon:

שִׁיר הַמַּעֲלוֹת, בְּשׁוּב יהוה אֶת שִׁיבַת צִיּוֹן, הָיִינוּ כְּחֹלְמִים. אָז יִמָּלֵא שְׂחוֹק פִּינוּ וּלְשׁוֹנֵנוּ רִנָּה, אָז יֹאמְרוּ בַגּוֹיִם, הִגְדִּיל יהוה לַעֲשׂוֹת עִם אֵלֶּה. הִגְדִּיל יהוה לַעֲשׂוֹת עִמָּנוּ, הָיִינוּ שְׂמֵחִים. שׁוּבָה יהוה אֶת שְׁבִיתֵנוּ, כַּאֲפִיקִים בַּנֶּגֶב. הַזֹּרְעִים בְּדִמְעָה בְּרִנָּה יִקְצֹרוּ. הָלוֹךְ יֵלֵךְ וּבָכֹה נֹשֵׂא מֶשֶׁךְ הַזָּרַע, בֹּא יָבֹא בְרִנָּה, נֹשֵׂא אֲלֻמֹּתָיו.

A song that the *Leviim* used to sing on the steps of the *Beis HaMikdash*: When Hashem will bring back the exiles to Eretz Yisrael, it will be like a dream come true. We will be filled with laughter and song. The other nations will declare, "Hashem has done great things for His people." Hashem has done great things for us — we will be happy. Hashem, please bring our people back to Eretz Yisrael, so it will be like a dry land that becomes filled with flowing springs. Let our people be like the farmers who plant seeds with tears, but are filled with joy when they harvest the crops. Let our people be like the one who cries when he carries his seeds to the field, but is joyous when he comes back carrying his bundles.

תְּהִלַּת יהוה יְדַבֶּר פִּי, וִיבָרֵךְ כָּל בָּשָׂר שֵׁם קָדְשׁוֹ לְעוֹלָם וָעֶד. וַאֲנַחְנוּ נְבָרֵךְ יָהּ, מֵעַתָּה וְעַד עוֹלָם, הַלְלוּיָהּ. הוֹדוּ לַיהוה כִּי טוֹב, כִּי לְעוֹלָם חַסְדּוֹ. מִי יְמַלֵּל גְּבוּרוֹת יהוה, יַשְׁמִיעַ כָּל תְּהִלָּתוֹ.

I will praise Hashem and may everyone bless Hashem forever. Let us give thanks to Hashem for He is good. He is always kind. Who can retell the miracles He does? Who can say all His praise?

If there are three or more males aged thirteen or older who have eaten together, one of them formally invites everyone to join in saying Bircas HaMazon. The leader of Bircas HaMazon begins his invitation:

רַבּוֹתַי נְבָרֵךְ

Gentlemen, let us bless.

Everyone else answers:

יְהִי שֵׁם יהוה מְבֹרָךְ מֵעַתָּה וְעַד עוֹלָם.

May Hashem's Name be blessed, from now to forever.

The leader continues (if ten men join, the words in brackets are included):

יְהִי שֵׁם יהוה מְבֹרָךְ מֵעַתָּה וְעַד עוֹלָם.

May Hashem's Name be blessed, from now to forever.

בִּרְשׁוּת מָרָנָן וְרַבָּנָן וְרַבּוֹתַי, נְבָרֵךְ [אֱלֹהֵינוּ] שֶׁאָכַלְנוּ מִשֶּׁלּוֹ.

With the permission of the honored people here, let us bless [our God] Whose food we have eaten.

Everyone else answers:

בָּרוּךְ [אֱלֹהֵינוּ] שֶׁאָכַלְנוּ מִשֶּׁלּוֹ וּבְטוּבוֹ חָיִינוּ.

Blessed is He [our God] from Whose food we have eaten and through Whose goodness we live.

The leader continues:

בָּרוּךְ [אֱלֹהֵינוּ] שֶׁאָכַלְנוּ מִשֶּׁלּוֹ וּבְטוּבוֹ חָיִינוּ.

Blessed is He [our God] from Whose food we have eaten and through Whose goodness we live.

All continue:

בָּרוּךְ הוּא וּבָרוּךְ שְׁמוֹ.

Blessed is He and blessed is His Name.

FIRST BLESSING

Blessed are You, Hashem, our God, King of the universe, Who feeds the entire world with His goodness, with love, with kindness, and with mercy. He gives food to everyone because His kindness is forever. Since He is so good, we have always had enough food. May He make sure that we always have enough food. We ask for this so that we can praise His great Name, because He is the God Who feeds everyone and does good for everyone. He prepares food for everything He has created. Blessed are You, Hashem, Who feeds everyone.

בָּרוּךְ אַתָּה יהוה אֱלֹהֵינוּ מֶלֶךְ הָעוֹלָם, הַזָּן אֶת הָעוֹלָם כֻּלּוֹ, בְּטוּבוֹ, בְּחֵן בְּחֶסֶד וּבְרַחֲמִים. הוּא נֹתֵן לֶחֶם לְכָל בָּשָׂר, כִּי לְעוֹלָם חַסְדּוֹ. וּבְטוּבוֹ הַגָּדוֹל, תָּמִיד לֹא חָסַר לָנוּ, וְאַל יֶחְסַר לָנוּ מָזוֹן לְעוֹלָם וָעֶד. בַּעֲבוּר שְׁמוֹ הַגָּדוֹל, כִּי הוּא אֵל זָן וּמְפַרְנֵס לַכֹּל, וּמֵטִיב לַכֹּל, וּמֵכִין מָזוֹן לְכָל בְּרִיּוֹתָיו אֲשֶׁר בָּרָא. בָּרוּךְ אַתָּה יהוה, הַזָּן אֶת הַכֹּל.

Did You Know??

Most *berachos* were written by the Sages. But there is one *berachah* that is commanded by the Torah — *Bircas HaMazon*. The Torah says, "You shall eat, you shall be satisfied, and you shall bless Hashem, your God."

There are four separate blessing in *Bircas HaMazon*.

The first blessing is called "*Bircas HaZan*," the *Blessing for the Food*. This *berachah* was written by Moshe to thank Hashem for giving the Jews the manna (מָן) to eat in the desert after they left Egypt.

A Closer Look

We leave some bread from the meal on the table when we say *Bircas HaMazon*.

SECOND BLESSING

We thank You, Hashem, our God, for giving Eretz Yisrael, a beautiful and good land, to our ancestors to be ours.

We thank You for taking us out of Egypt where we were slaves; for the mitzvah of *bris milah*; for teaching us Your Torah, for the mitzvos that You told us; and for the life, love, and kindness that you have given us; and for the food You prepare for us every day, always.

נוֹדֶה לְךָ, יהוה אֱלֹהֵינוּ, עַל שֶׁהִנְחַלְתָּ לַאֲבוֹתֵינוּ אֶרֶץ חֶמְדָּה טוֹבָה וּרְחָבָה. וְעַל שֶׁהוֹצֵאתָנוּ יהוה אֱלֹהֵינוּ מֵאֶרֶץ מִצְרַיִם, וּפְדִיתָנוּ מִבֵּית עֲבָדִים, וְעַל בְּרִיתְךָ שֶׁחָתַמְתָּ בִּבְשָׂרֵנוּ, וְעַל תּוֹרָתְךָ שֶׁלִּמַּדְתָּנוּ, וְעַל חֻקֶּיךָ שֶׁהוֹדַעְתָּנוּ, וְעַל חַיִּים חֵן וָחֶסֶד שֶׁחוֹנַנְתָּנוּ, וְעַל אֲכִילַת מָזוֹן שָׁאַתָּה זָן וּמְפַרְנֵס אוֹתָנוּ תָּמִיד, בְּכָל יוֹם וּבְכָל עֵת וּבְכָל שָׁעָה.

Did You Know??
This is the second blessing of *Bircas HaMazon*. It is called "*Bircas HaAretz*," the *Blessing of the Land of Israel*. We thank Hashem for giving us Eretz Yisrael and the mitzvos of the Torah. This *berachah* was written by Yehoshua, who led the Jewish people into Eretz Yisrael.

A Closer Look
A *berachah* puts holiness into ordinary things. It makes food and drink the tools that draw us closer to Hashem.

Al HaNissim / עַל הַנִּסִּים

On Chanukah and Purim we add the following:

(וְ)עַל הַנִּסִּים וְעַל הַפֻּרְקָן וְעַל הַגְּבוּרוֹת וְעַל הַתְּשׁוּעוֹת וְעַל הַמִּלְחָמוֹת שֶׁעָשִׂיתָ לַאֲבוֹתֵינוּ בַּיָּמִים הָהֵם בַּזְּמַן הַזֶּה.

And (we thank Hashem) for the miracles, and for saving us, and for the victories in the wars, which You did for our fathers, in those days, in this time of the year.

A Closer Look

Purim and Chanukah are holidays that came after the Torah was given. Chanukah marks the time when the Jews freed the *Beis HaMikdash* from the Syrian-Greeks; our people were able to light the Menorah and we became free to do mitzvos again. Before Purim, the Jews were saved from the wicked decrees of Haman, who tried to destroy the entire Jewish nation.

Our enemies knew that if they wanted to destroy us they must stop us from learning Torah and following Hashem's laws. This can never happen, because Hashem promised that the Jewish People will never be destroyed and Torah will never be forgotten.

On Chanukah we add the following:

בִּימֵי מַתִּתְיָהוּ בֶּן יוֹחָנָן כֹּהֵן גָּדוֹל חַשְׁמוֹנָאִי וּבָנָיו, כְּשֶׁעָמְדָה מַלְכוּת יָוָן הָרְשָׁעָה עַל עַמְּךָ יִשְׂרָאֵל, לְהַשְׁכִּיחָם תּוֹרָתֶךָ, וּלְהַעֲבִירָם מֵחֻקֵּי רְצוֹנֶךָ. וְאַתָּה בְּרַחֲמֶיךָ הָרַבִּים, עָמַדְתָּ לָהֶם בְּעֵת צָרָתָם, רַבְתָּ אֶת רִיבָם, דַּנְתָּ אֶת דִּינָם, נָקַמְתָּ אֶת נִקְמָתָם. מָסַרְתָּ גִבּוֹרִים בְּיַד חַלָּשִׁים, וְרַבִּים בְּיַד מְעַטִּים, וּטְמֵאִים בְּיַד טְהוֹרִים, וּרְשָׁעִים בְּיַד צַדִּיקִים, וְזֵדִים בְּיַד עוֹסְקֵי תוֹרָתֶךָ, וּלְךָ עָשִׂיתָ שֵׁם גָּדוֹל וְקָדוֹשׁ בְּעוֹלָמֶךָ, וּלְעַמְּךָ יִשְׂרָאֵל עָשִׂיתָ תְּשׁוּעָה גְדוֹלָה וּפֻרְקָן כְּהַיּוֹם הַזֶּה. וְאַחַר כֵּן בָּאוּ בָנֶיךָ לִדְבִיר בֵּיתֶךָ, וּפִנּוּ אֶת הֵיכָלֶךָ, וְטִהֲרוּ אֶת מִקְדָּשֶׁךָ, וְהִדְלִיקוּ נֵרוֹת בְּחַצְרוֹת קָדְשֶׁךָ, וְקָבְעוּ שְׁמוֹנַת יְמֵי חֲנֻכָּה אֵלוּ, לְהוֹדוֹת וּלְהַלֵּל לְשִׁמְךָ הַגָּדוֹל.

I n the days of Mattisyahu the son of Yochanan the *Kohen*, the Chashmonean, and his sons. The evil Greek kingdom stood against Your nation, and tried to make them forget Your Torah, and tried to force them not to follow Your laws.

And You, with Your great mercy, stood up for the Jews in their time of suffering. You listened to them and took revenge for them. You gave the strong (Greeks) into the hands of the weak (Jewish people); the many into the hands of the few; the impure into the hands of the pure; the wicked ones into the hands of the *tzaddikim*; and the evil ones into the hands of the ones who study Your Torah. You made Your Name great and holy in Your world. And as for Your nation, Israel, You made for them a great victory and a salvation which lasts until today. Afterwards, Your children came to Your *Beis HaMikdash* and to the Holy of Holies, purified Your Temple, and lit the lamps in the yard of Your Holy Place. And they established these eight days of Chanukah, in order to give thanks and to praise Your great Name.

On Purim we add the following:

בִּימֵי מָרְדְּכַי וְאֶסְתֵּר בְּשׁוּשַׁן הַבִּירָה, כְּשֶׁעָמַד עֲלֵיהֶם הָמָן הָרָשָׁע, בִּקֵּשׁ לְהַשְׁמִיד לַהֲרֹג וּלְאַבֵּד אֶת כָּל הַיְּהוּדִים, מִנַּעַר וְעַד זָקֵן, טַף וְנָשִׁים בְּיוֹם אֶחָד, בִּשְׁלוֹשָׁה עָשָׂר לְחֹדֶשׁ שְׁנֵים עָשָׂר, הוּא חֹדֶשׁ אֲדָר, וּשְׁלָלָם לָבוֹז. וְאַתָּה בְּרַחֲמֶיךָ הָרַבִּים הֵפַרְתָּ אֶת עֲצָתוֹ, וְקִלְקַלְתָּ אֶת מַחֲשַׁבְתּוֹ, וַהֲשֵׁבוֹתָ לּוֹ גְּמוּלוֹ בְּרֹאשׁוֹ, וְתָלוּ אוֹתוֹ וְאֶת בָּנָיו עַל הָעֵץ.

I n the days of Mordechai and Esther in the capital city of Shushan, the evil Haman stood up against the Jews and tried to destroy them. He wanted to kill all the Jews, young and old, babies and women, all on the same day, on the thirteenth day of Adar, the twelfth month, and steal all they owned.

But You, with Your great mercy, stopped him and caused everything he wanted to do to the Jewish people to happen to him instead. And so they hanged Haman and his sons from the tree.

וְעַל הַכֹּל יהוה אֱלֹהֵינוּ, אֲנַחְנוּ מוֹדִים לָךְ וּמְבָרְכִים אוֹתָךְ, יִתְבָּרַךְ שִׁמְךָ בְּפִי כָּל חַי תָּמִיד לְעוֹלָם וָעֶד. כַּכָּתוּב, וְאָכַלְתָּ וְשָׂבָעְתָּ, וּבֵרַכְתָּ אֶת יהוה אֱלֹהֶיךָ, עַל הָאָרֶץ הַטֹּבָה אֲשֶׁר נָתַן לָךְ. בָּרוּךְ אַתָּה יהוה, עַל הָאָרֶץ וְעַל הַמָּזוֹן.

For everything, Hashem, our God, we thank You and bless You.

May Your Name always be blessed by everyone, as it is written in the Torah, "You will eat, you will be satisfied, and then you will bless Hashem, your God, for the good land that He gave you." Blessed are You, Hashem, for the land and for the food.

Did You Know??
This is the last part of the second blessing. Yehoshua wrote this when he led the Jews into Eretz Yisrael because now the Jews began to eat food grown from the land. Until this point, they had been eating manna in the desert.

A Closer Look
Whenever you make a *berachah*, you are showing that you believe in Hashem and depend on him for everything you do and receive.

THIRD BLESSING

רַחֵם יהוה אֱלֹהֵינוּ עַל יִשְׂרָאֵל עַמֶּךָ, וְעַל יְרוּשָׁלַיִם עִירֶךָ, וְעַל צִיּוֹן מִשְׁכַּן כְּבוֹדֶךָ, וְעַל מַלְכוּת בֵּית דָּוִד מְשִׁיחֶךָ, וְעַל הַבַּיִת הַגָּדוֹל וְהַקָּדוֹשׁ שֶׁנִּקְרָא שִׁמְךָ עָלָיו. אֱלֹהֵינוּ אָבִינוּ, רְעֵנוּ זוּנֵנוּ פַּרְנְסֵנוּ וְכַלְכְּלֵנוּ וְהַרְוִיחֵנוּ, וְהַרְוַח לָנוּ יהוה אֱלֹהֵינוּ מְהֵרָה מִכָּל צָרוֹתֵינוּ. וְנָא אַל תַּצְרִיכֵנוּ, יהוה אֱלֹהֵינוּ, לֹא לִידֵי מַתְּנַת בָּשָׂר וָדָם, וְלֹא לִידֵי הַלְוָאָתָם, כִּי אִם לְיָדְךָ הַמְּלֵאָה הַפְּתוּחָה הַקְּדוֹשָׁה וְהָרְחָבָה, שֶׁלֹּא נֵבוֹשׁ וְלֹא נִכָּלֵם לְעוֹלָם וָעֶד.

Hashem, our God, please have mercy on Your nation Israel; on Jerusalem, Your city; on the Temple Mount, the place of Your Glory; on the kingdom of David, Your king; and on the holy *Beis HaMikdash* which is called by Your Name. Our God, our Father, take care of us, feed us, support us, give us what we need, and make our lives easier. Hashem, our God, give us relief now from our troubles. Please, Hashem, our God, don't make us need gifts or even loans from other people; let us get all our needs from Your hand, which is open, holy, and generous. Then we will never feel ashamed or embarrassed.

A Closer Look
This is the beginning of the third blessing. It is called *"Bircas Binyan Yerushalayim," the Blessing of the Building of Jerusalem*. We ask Hashem to have mercy on us and to rebuild Jerusalem and the *Beis HaMikdash*.

On Sabbos we recite this paragraph:

רְצֵה וְהַחֲלִיצֵנוּ יהוה אֱלֹהֵינוּ בְּמִצְוֹתֶיךָ, וּבְמִצְוַת יוֹם הַשְּׁבִיעִי הַשַּׁבָּת הַגָּדוֹל וְהַקָּדוֹשׁ הַזֶּה, כִּי יוֹם זֶה גָּדוֹל וְקָדוֹשׁ הוּא לְפָנֶיךָ, לִשְׁבָּת בּוֹ וְלָנוּחַ בּוֹ בְּאַהֲבָה כְּמִצְוַת רְצוֹנֶךָ. וּבִרְצוֹנְךָ הָנִיחַ לָנוּ, יהוה אֱלֹהֵינוּ, שֶׁלֹּא תְהֵא צָרָה וְיָגוֹן וַאֲנָחָה בְּיוֹם מְנוּחָתֵנוּ. וְהַרְאֵנוּ יהוה אֱלֹהֵינוּ בְּנֶחָמַת צִיּוֹן עִירֶךָ, וּבְבִנְיַן יְרוּשָׁלַיִם עִיר קָדְשֶׁךָ, כִּי אַתָּה הוּא בַּעַל הַיְשׁוּעוֹת וּבַעַל הַנֶּחָמוֹת.

Please Hashem, our God, make us strong through Your mitzvos and through this special mitzvah of the great and holy Shabbos. This is a great and holy day for us to rest on, as You have commanded. Please, Hashem, our God, calm us, and let there not be any trouble or sadness on this day of rest. Hashem, let us see Your city Zion comforted. Let us see Your holy city Jerusalem being rebuilt, because only You have the power to help and to comfort.

A Closer Look
Hashem created the world in six days and on the seventh day (Shabbos) He rested. It is a spiritual day, a day when we can forget about all our worries and just concentrate on connecting with Hashem. On Shabbos we should think about everything Hashem has done for us, and continues to do every day.

On Rosh Chodesh and Holidays we add the following paragraph:

אֱלֹהֵינוּ וֵאלֹהֵי אֲבוֹתֵינוּ, יַעֲלֶה, וְיָבֹא, וְיַגִּיעַ, וְיֵרָאֶה, וְיֵרָצֶה, וְיִשָּׁמַע, וְיִפָּקֵד, וְיִזָּכֵר, זִכְרוֹנֵנוּ וּפִקְדוֹנֵנוּ, וְזִכְרוֹן אֲבוֹתֵינוּ, וְזִכְרוֹן מָשִׁיחַ בֶּן דָּוִד עַבְדֶּךָ, וְזִכְרוֹן יְרוּשָׁלַיִם עִיר קָדְשֶׁךָ, וְזִכְרוֹן כָּל עַמְּךָ בֵּית יִשְׂרָאֵל לְפָנֶיךָ, לִפְלֵיטָה לְטוֹבָה לְחֵן וּלְחֶסֶד וּלְרַחֲמִים, לְחַיִּים וּלְשָׁלוֹם, בְּיוֹם

Our God and God of our fathers, we pray that the following thoughts will be heard and recalled by You: memories of us; of our fathers; of Mashiach, from the family of David; of Jerusalem, Your holy city; and of the entire nation of Israel. Remember all these to rescue us, to give us goodness, love, and kindness, life and peace, on this day of

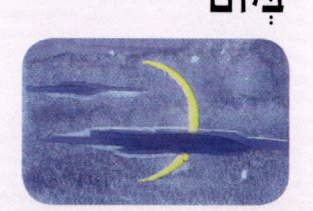

on Rosh Chodesh say:
Rosh Chodesh. רֹאשׁ הַחֹדֶשׁ הַזֶּה.

on Pesach say:
the Festival of Matzos. חַג הַמַּצּוֹת הַזֶּה.

on Shavuos say:
the Shavuos Festival. חַג הַשָּׁבֻעוֹת הַזֶּה.

on Rosh Hashanah say:
Remembrance. הַזִּכָּרוֹן הַזֶּה.

on Succos say:
the Succos Festival. חַג הַסֻּכּוֹת הַזֶּה.

on Shemini Atzeres and Simchas Torah say:
the Shemini Atzeres Festival. הַשְּׁמִינִי חַג הָעֲצֶרֶת הַזֶּה.

Remember us, Hashem, our God, for good, for blessing, and for life. Have pity on us and save us, because we look to You for help since you are the generous God, filled with mercy.

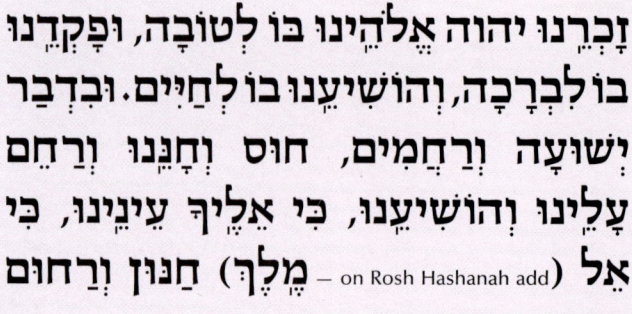

זָכְרֵנוּ יהוה אֱלֹהֵינוּ בּוֹ לְטוֹבָה, וּפָקְדֵנוּ בּוֹ לִבְרָכָה, וְהוֹשִׁיעֵנוּ בוֹ לְחַיִּים. וּבִדְבַר יְשׁוּעָה וְרַחֲמִים, חוּס וְחָנֵּנוּ וְרַחֵם עָלֵינוּ וְהוֹשִׁיעֵנוּ, כִּי אֵלֶיךָ עֵינֵינוּ, כִּי אֵל (מֶלֶךְ — *on Rosh Hashanah add*) חַנּוּן וְרַחוּם אָתָּה.

> **Did You Know??** 
> We say *Ya'aleh Ve'yavo* not only in *Bircas HaMazon*, but also in *Shemoneh Esrei* on festivals and Rosh Chodesh.
> It was written by our Sages almost 2000 years ago. It is a request to Hashem to remember us for good things, just as He did many years ago in the time of the *Avos*, and in the time of the *Beis HaMikdash*, when we brought special offerings on the festivals and Rosh Chodesh.

And please rebuild Jerusalem, the Holy City, quickly, in our lifetime. Blessed are You, Hashem, Who builds Jerusalem (with His mercy). Amen.

וּבְנֵה יְרוּשָׁלַיִם עִיר הַקֹּדֶשׁ בִּמְהֵרָה בְיָמֵינוּ. בָּרוּךְ אַתָּה יהוה, בּוֹנֵה (בְּרַחֲמָיו) יְרוּשָׁלָיִם. אָמֵן.

Did You Know??
The *Beis HaMikdash* was Hashem's resting place in our world. It is where we were closest to Hashem, the place where He received our offerings. The place where the *Beis HaMikdash* stood is the point that connects our physical world with the spiritual world above. Now, all we have left is one wall — the *Kosel*, the wall that surrounded the Temple Mount. But we pray every day for Hashem to rebuild Jerusalem and to rebuild the *Beis HaMikdash*.

FOURTH BLESSING

Blessed are You, Hashem, our God, King of the universe, God Who is our Father, our King, our Master; Who created us, Who saved us, Who made us; our Holy One, the Holy One of Yaakov our forefather; our Shepherd, the Shepherd of Israel; the King Who is good and Who does good to everyone. Every single day He *did* good, He *does* good, and He *will do* good for us. He *gave* us much, He *gives* us much, and He *will give* us much forever; with love, kindness, and with much help, success, blessing, comfort, support, mercy, life, and peace. May we never lack any good things.

בָּרוּךְ אַתָּה יהוה אֱלֹהֵינוּ מֶלֶךְ הָעוֹלָם, הָאֵל אָבִינוּ מַלְכֵּנוּ אַדִירֵנוּ בּוֹרְאֵנוּ גּוֹאֲלֵנוּ יוֹצְרֵנוּ. קְדוֹשֵׁנוּ קְדוֹשׁ יַעֲקֹב, רוֹעֵנוּ רוֹעֵה יִשְׂרָאֵל, הַמֶּלֶךְ הַטּוֹב וְהַמֵּטִיב לַכֹּל, שֶׁבְּכָל יוֹם וָיוֹם הוּא הֵטִיב, הוּא מֵטִיב, הוּא יֵיטִיב לָנוּ. הוּא גְמָלָנוּ, הוּא גוֹמְלֵנוּ, הוּא יִגְמְלֵנוּ לָעַד, לְחֵן וּלְחֶסֶד וּלְרַחֲמִים וּלְרֶוַח הַצָּלָה וְהַצְלָחָה, בְּרָכָה וִישׁוּעָה נֶחָמָה פַּרְנָסָה וְכַלְכָּלָה וְרַחֲמִים וְחַיִּים וְשָׁלוֹם וְכָל טוֹב, וּמִכָּל טוּב לְעוֹלָם אַל יְחַסְּרֵנוּ.

A Closer Look

This is the fourth blessing. It is called "HaTov VeHametiv," *Who is good and does good*. We thank Hashem because He has always been good to us, He is still good to us, and He will always be good to us.

Did You Know??

The Sages wrote this blessing to thank Hashem for a miracle after the Second *Beis HaMikdash* was destroyed. The Romans killed many Jews in the city of Beitar and would not let them be buried for years. Hashem made a miracle. The bodies were still fresh when the Jews finally buried them. This *berachah* was written when the people who were killed by the Romans in Beitar were finally buried.

24

We now make various requests of Hashem:

הָרַחֲמָן הוּא יִמְלוֹךְ עָלֵינוּ לְעוֹלָם וָעֶד. הָרַחֲמָן הוּא יִתְבָּרַךְ בַּשָּׁמַיִם וּבָאָרֶץ. הָרַחֲמָן הוּא יִשְׁתַּבַּח לְדוֹר דּוֹרִים, וְיִתְפָּאַר בָּנוּ לָעַד וּלְנֵצַח נְצָחִים, וְיִתְהַדַּר בָּנוּ לָעַד וּלְעוֹלְמֵי עוֹלָמִים. הָרַחֲמָן הוּא יְפַרְנְסֵנוּ בְּכָבוֹד. הָרַחֲמָן הוּא יִשְׁבּוֹר עֻלֵּנוּ מֵעַל צַוָּארֵנוּ, וְהוּא יוֹלִיכֵנוּ קוֹמְמִיּוּת לְאַרְצֵנוּ. הָרַחֲמָן הוּא יִשְׁלַח לָנוּ בְּרָכָה מְרֻבָּה בַּבַּיִת הַזֶּה, וְעַל שֻׁלְחָן זֶה שֶׁאָכַלְנוּ עָלָיו. הָרַחֲמָן הוּא יִשְׁלַח לָנוּ אֶת אֵלִיָּהוּ הַנָּבִיא זָכוּר לַטּוֹב, וִיבַשֶּׂר לָנוּ בְּשׂוֹרוֹת טוֹבוֹת יְשׁוּעוֹת וְנֶחָמוֹת.

May the Merciful God always be our King. May the Merciful God be blessed in heaven and on earth. May the Merciful God be praised in every generation, and always be proud of us and honored by the way we act. May the Merciful God support us with honor. May the Merciful God stop all our suffering and lead our proudly to our land, Eretz Yisrael. May the Merciful God send much blessing into this house and on this table upon which we have eaten. May the Merciful God send us Eliyahu the Prophet, who is remembered for doing good, and may he bring us good news, to save us and comfort us.

The Talmud tells us that a guest should recite the following in honor of his host:

יְהִי רָצוֹן שֶׁלֹּא יֵבוֹשׁ וְלֹא יִכָּלֵם בַּעַל הַבַּיִת הַזֶּה, לֹא בָּעוֹלָם הַזֶּה וְלֹא בָּעוֹלָם הַבָּא, וְיַצְלִיחַ בְּכָל נְכָסָיו, וְיִהְיוּ נְכָסָיו מֻצְלָחִים וּקְרוֹבִים לָעִיר, וְאַל יִשְׁלוֹט שָׂטָן בְּמַעֲשֵׂה יָדָיו, וְאַל יִזְדַּקֵּק לְפָנָיו שׁוּם דְּבַר חֵטְא וְהִרְהוּר עָוֹן, מֵעַתָּה וְעַד עוֹלָם.

May it be God's will that this host not be embarrassed either in this world or in the World to Come. May he be successful in everything that he does and may it be easy for him to earn a living. May he never be led into sin or into wicked thought.

People eating in their parents' house say:

הָרַחֲמָן הוּא יְבָרֵךְ אֶת אָבִי מוֹרִי בַּעַל הַבַּיִת הַזֶּה, וְאֶת אִמִּי מוֹרָתִי בַּעֲלַת הַבַּיִת הַזֶּה, אוֹתָם וְאֶת בֵּיתָם וְאֶת זַרְעָם וְאֶת כָּל אֲשֶׁר לָהֶם.

May the merciful God bless my father and teacher, the head of this house, and my mother and teacher, the lady of this house; may He bless them, their home, their children, and everything they have,

Adults eating in their own house say (including the words in parentheses that apply):

הָרַחֲמָן הוּא יְבָרֵךְ אוֹתִי (וְאֶת אִשְׁתִּי / וְאֶת בַּעֲלִי, וְאֶת זַרְעִי) וְאֶת כָּל אֲשֶׁר לִי.

May the Merciful God bless me (and my spouse and my children) and all that is mine,

People eating in someone else's house say:

הָרַחֲמָן הוּא יְבָרֵךְ אֶת בַּעַל הַבַּיִת הַזֶּה, וְאֶת בַּעֲלַת הַבַּיִת הַזֶּה, אוֹתָם וְאֶת בֵּיתָם וְאֶת זַרְעָם וְאֶת כָּל אֲשֶׁר לָהֶם.

May the Merciful God bless the head of this house and the lady of this house; may He bless them, their home, their children, and everything they have,

All continue here:

אוֹתָנוּ וְאֶת כָּל אֲשֶׁר לָנוּ, כְּמוֹ שֶׁנִּתְבָּרְכוּ אֲבוֹתֵינוּ אַבְרָהָם יִצְחָק וְיַעֲקֹב בַּכֹּל מִכֹּל כֹּל, כֵּן יְבָרֵךְ אוֹתָנוּ כֻּלָּנוּ יַחַד בִּבְרָכָה שְׁלֵמָה וְנֹאמַר, אָמֵן.

us, and everything that we have, just as our forefathers Avraham, Yitzchak, and Yaakov were blessed with everything, may He bless us also with everything. Amen.

בַּמָּרוֹם יְלַמְּדוּ עֲלֵיהֶם וְעָלֵינוּ זְכוּת, שֶׁתְּהֵא לְמִשְׁמֶרֶת שָׁלוֹם. וְנִשָּׂא בְרָכָה מֵאֵת יהוה, וּצְדָקָה מֵאֱלֹהֵי יִשְׁעֵנוּ, וְנִמְצָא חֵן וְשֵׂכֶל טוֹב בְּעֵינֵי אֱלֹהִים וְאָדָם.

In heaven above, may we and everyone with us be judged as deserving of peace. May we get a blessing and kindness from Hashem, and may Hashem and other people look at us with favor and with understanding.

On Shabbos we add:

הָרַחֲמָן הוּא יַנְחִילֵנוּ יוֹם שֶׁכֻּלּוֹ שַׁבָּת וּמְנוּחָה לְחַיֵּי הָעוֹלָמִים.

May the Merciful God let us inherit the World to Come, which is a day that is all Shabbos, a day of complete rest, forever.

On Rosh Chodesh we add:

הָרַחֲמָן הוּא יְחַדֵּשׁ עָלֵינוּ אֶת הַחֹדֶשׁ הַזֶּה לְטוֹבָה וְלִבְרָכָה.

May the Merciful God renew this month with goodness and blessing.

On Holidays we add:

הָרַחֲמָן הוּא יַנְחִילֵנוּ יוֹם שֶׁכֻּלּוֹ טוֹב.

May the Merciful God let us inherit a day which is completely good.

On Rosh Hashanah we add:

הָרַחֲמָן הוּא יְחַדֵּשׁ עָלֵינוּ אֶת הַשָּׁנָה הַזֹּאת לְטוֹבָה וְלִבְרָכָה.

May the Merciful God renew this year with goodness and blessing.

On Succos we add:

הָרַחֲמָן הוּא יָקִים לָנוּ אֶת סֻכַּת דָּוִיד הַנֹּפֶלֶת.

May the Merciful God build for us King David's fallen *succah* (the *Beis HaMikdash*).

הָרַחֲמָן הוּא יְזַכֵּנוּ לִימוֹת הַמָּשִׁיחַ וּלְחַיֵּי הָעוֹלָם הַבָּא.

May the Merciful God let us live until the Mashiach comes, and let us earn the life of the World to Come.

מַגְדִּל — *On weekdays we say*

מִגְדּוֹל — *On Shabbos, Rosh Chodesh, and Holidays we say*

יְשׁוּעוֹת מַלְכּוֹ וְעֹשֶׂה חֶסֶד לִמְשִׁיחוֹ לְדָוִד וּלְזַרְעוֹ עַד עוֹלָם. עֹשֶׂה שָׁלוֹם בִּמְרוֹמָיו, הוּא יַעֲשֶׂה שָׁלוֹם עָלֵינוּ וְעַל כָּל יִשְׂרָאֵל. וְאִמְרוּ, אָמֵן.

On weekdays we say:
Hashem performs great salvations and shows

On Shabbos, Rosh Chodesh, and Holidays we say:
Hashem is a tower of help and performs great

kindness towards King David and his descendants forever. Hashem, Who makes peace in His Heavens, should please make peace for us and for all of Israel. Now respond, Amen.

יְראוּ אֶת יהוה קְדֹשָׁיו, כִּי אֵין מַחְסוֹר לִירֵאָיו. כְּפִירִים רָשׁוּ וְרָעֵבוּ, וְדֹרְשֵׁי יהוה לֹא יַחְסְרוּ כָל טוֹב. הוֹדוּ לַיהוה כִּי טוֹב, כִּי לְעוֹלָם חַסְדּוֹ. פּוֹתֵחַ אֶת יָדֶךָ, וּמַשְׂבִּיעַ לְכָל חַי רָצוֹן. בָּרוּךְ הַגֶּבֶר אֲשֶׁר יִבְטַח בַּיהוה, וְהָיָה יהוה מִבְטַחוֹ. נַעַר הָיִיתִי גַּם זָקַנְתִּי, וְלֹא רָאִיתִי צַדִּיק נֶעֱזָב, וְזַרְעוֹ מְבַקֶּשׁ לָחֶם. יהוה עֹז לְעַמּוֹ יִתֵּן, יהוה יְבָרֵךְ אֶת עַמּוֹ בַשָּׁלוֹם.

You, who are holy to Hashem, should fear Him, because those who fear Him do not need anything. Even strong young lions may go hungry, but if you try to be close to Hashem you will not miss anything that is good for you. Thank Hashem for He is good, and His kindness lasts forever. Please God, open up Your Hand and give everyone all that they desire. Blessed is the person who trusts in Hashem — for Hashem will protect him. I was young and now I am old, and in all my years, I never saw a *tzaddik* who was all alone and whose children had to beg for food. Hashem will give strength to His nation, Hashem will bless His nation with peace.

26

Borei Nefashos / בּוֹרֵא נְפָשׁוֹת

After eating or drinking any food that is not followed by either Bircas HaMazon or Al HaMichyah (or Al HaGefen or Al Ha'Etz), you say:

בָּרוּךְ אַתָּה יהוה אֱלֹהֵינוּ מֶלֶךְ הָעוֹלָם, בּוֹרֵא נְפָשׁוֹת רַבּוֹת וְחֶסְרוֹנָן, עַל כָּל מַה שֶּׁבָּרָא(תָ) לְהַחֲיוֹת בָּהֶם נֶפֶשׁ כָּל חָי. בָּרוּךְ חֵי הָעוֹלָמִים.

Blessed are You, Hashem, our God, King of the universe, Who creates many living things with various needs. You keep alive whatever You create and provide them with whatever they need. Blessed is He, the life of the worlds.

Did You Know??

The Torah teaches us that we must thank Hashem after we eat a meal. That is why we say *Bircas HaMazon*. Our Rabbis understand from this that not only should we say a *berachah* after eating a meal with bread, but we should say a *berachah* after everything we eat.

Al HaMichyah / עַל הַמִּחְיָה
Bircas Me'ein Shalosh / בִּרְכַּת מֵעֵין שָׁלשׁ

You say this blessing after eating a certain minimum amount of 1) grains (such as cake or cereal), 2) wine or grape juice, 3) grapes, 4) figs, 5) pomegranates, 6) olives, or 7) dates

Blessed are You, Hashem, our God, King of the universe, בָּרוּךְ אַתָּה יהוה אֱלֹהֵינוּ מֶלֶךְ הָעוֹלָם,

After grains (such as cake or cereal):
for the nourishment and basic food, עַל הַמִּחְיָה וְעַל הַכַּלְכָּלָה,

After wine or grape juice:
for the grapevine and the fruit of the grapevine, [וְ]עַל הַגֶּפֶן וְעַל פְּרִי הַגֶּפֶן,

After fruits (such as grapes, figs, pomegranates, olives or dates):
for the tree and the fruit of the tree, [וְ]עַל הָעֵץ וְעַל פְּרִי הָעֵץ,

Did You Know??
We make the *berachah* Al HaMichyah (*Bircas Me'ein Shalosh*) after eating one of the the *Shivas HaMinim*, the *Seven Special Types of Food* that Eretz Yisrael is especially blessed with. These are foods for which the Torah praises Eretz Yisrael. They are: wheat, barley (including oats, rye, and spelt), grapes (including wine), figs, pomegranates, olives, and dates. You can see a picture of each of the *Shivas HaMinim* on page 30.

A Closer Look
Me'ein Shalosh means that this blessing has three parts. It mentions the main ideas of the first three blessings of *Bircas HaMazon*.

וְעַל תְּנוּבַת הַשָּׂדֶה, וְעַל אֶרֶץ חֶמְדָּה טוֹבָה וּרְחָבָה, שֶׁרָצִיתָ וְהִנְחַלְתָּ לַאֲבוֹתֵינוּ, לֶאֱכוֹל מִפִּרְיָהּ וְלִשְׂבּוֹעַ מִטּוּבָהּ. רַחֶם נָא יהוה אֱלֹהֵינוּ עַל יִשְׂרָאֵל עַמֶּךָ, וְעַל יְרוּשָׁלַיִם עִירֶךָ, וְעַל צִיּוֹן מִשְׁכַּן כְּבוֹדֶךָ, וְעַל מִזְבְּחֶךָ וְעַל הֵיכָלֶךָ. וּבְנֵה יְרוּשָׁלַיִם עִיר הַקֹּדֶשׁ בִּמְהֵרָה בְיָמֵינוּ, וְהַעֲלֵנוּ לְתוֹכָהּ, וְשַׂמְּחֵנוּ בְּבִנְיָנָהּ, וְנֹאכַל מִפִּרְיָהּ, וְנִשְׂבַּע מִטּוּבָהּ, וּנְבָרֶכְךָ עָלֶיהָ בִּקְדֻשָּׁה וּבְטָהֳרָה.

and for all the food grown in the field. And for the wonderful, good land that You gave to our fathers, to eat from its fruit, and to be satisfied from its goodness. Our God, have pity on Israel, Your nation, and on Jerusalem, Your city, and on Your Altar, and on Your *Beis HaMikdash*. Rebuild Jerusalem, the holy city, quickly, in our lifetime. Bring us to Jerusalem, and make us happy by rebuilding it. And let us eat the fruit of Eretz Yisrael and be satisfied with its goodness, and let us bless You for its holiness and purity.

On Shabbos we add:
וּרְצֵה וְהַחֲלִיצֵנוּ בְּיוֹם הַשַּׁבָּת הַזֶּה.
Please, let us rest on this day of Shabbos.

On Rosh Chodesh we add:
וְזָכְרֵנוּ (לְטוֹבָה) בְּיוֹם רֹאשׁ הַחֹדֶשׁ הַזֶּה.
And remember us on this day of Rosh Chodesh.

On Pesach we add:
וְשַׂמְּחֵנוּ בְּיוֹם חַג הַמַּצּוֹת הַזֶּה.
And make us happy on this Holiday of Matzos (Pesach).

On Shavuos we add:
וְשַׂמְּחֵנוּ בְּיוֹם חַג הַשָּׁבוּעוֹת הַזֶּה.
And make us happy on this Holiday of Shavuos.

On Succos we add:
וְשַׂמְּחֵנוּ בְּיוֹם חַג הַסֻּכּוֹת הַזֶּה.
And make us happy on this holiday of Succos.

On Shemini Atzeres/Simchas Torah we add:
וְשַׂמְּחֵנוּ בְּיוֹם הַשְּׁמִינִי חַג הָעֲצֶרֶת הַזֶּה.
And make us happy on this Holiday of Shemini Atzeres.

On Rosh Hashanah we add:
וְזָכְרֵנוּ לְטוֹבָה בְּיוֹם הַזִּכָּרוֹן הַזֶּה.
And remember us on this day of remembrance.

כִּי אַתָּה יהוה טוֹב וּמֵטִיב לַכֹּל, וְנוֹדֶה לְךָ

Because You, Hashem, are good, and do good to others, and we thank You

After grains (such as cake or cereal):
עַל הָאָרֶץ וְעַל הַמִּחְיָה.
for the land and for the nourishment.

After wine or grape juice:
עַל הָאָרֶץ וְעַל פְּרִי הַגָּפֶן.
for the land and the fruit of the grapevine.

After fruits (such as grapes, figs, pomegranates, olives or dates):
עַל הָאָרֶץ וְעַל הַפֵּרוֹת.
for the land and the fruits.

בָּרוּךְ אַתָּה יהוה,
Blessed are You, Hashem,

After grains (such as cake or cereal):
עַל הָאָרֶץ וְעַל הַמִּחְיָה.
for the land and for the nourishment.

After wine or grape juice:
עַל הָאָרֶץ וְעַל פְּרִי הַגָּפֶן.
for the land and the fruit of the grapevine.

After fruits (such as grapes, figs, pomegranates, olives or dates):
עַל הָאָרֶץ וְעַל הַפֵּרוֹת.
for the land and the fruits.

Shivas HaMinim / שִׁבְעַת הַמִינִים

Eretz Yisrael is especially blessed with Seven Special Types of Food. These are called the Shivas HaMinim.

Did You Know??
If you have many different foods to choose from, you should say the *berachah* first on one of these seven special types.

BARLEY / שעורה

WHEAT / חטה

OLIVES / זית

GRAPES / גפן

POMEGRANATES / רמון

FIGS / תאנה

DATES / תמר

30

Section 2

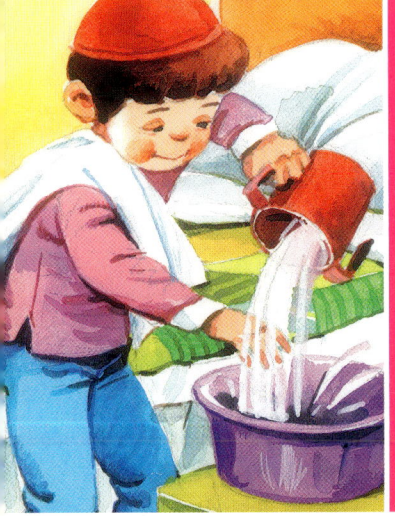

בִּרְכַּת הַמִּצְוֹות
Bircas HaMitzvos

Berachos on doing mitzvos.

Netilas Yadayim / נְטִילַת יָדַיִם

As soon as you wake up in the morning, wash "Netilas Yadayim," and go to the bathroom, you say the following berachah and Asher Yatzar (p. 40). Some people say these berachos as soon as they have washed and gone to the bathroom. Most people say them when they are ready to start Shacharis. You also say Al Netilas Yadayim when you wash your hands before you eat bread.

Blessed are You, Hashem, our God, King of the universe, Who has made us holy with His mitzvos, and commanded us about washing our hands.

בָּרוּךְ אַתָּה יהוה אֱלֹהֵינוּ מֶלֶךְ הָעוֹלָם, אֲשֶׁר קִדְּשָׁנוּ בְּמִצְוֹתָיו, וְצִוָּנוּ עַל נְטִילַת יָדָיִם.

Did You Know??

When you wash your hands in the morning it reminds you that the *Kohanim* washed their hands in the *Beis HaMikdash* before starting thier service in the *Beis HaMikdash*.

Our Rabbis teach us that you should say 100 *berachos* every day.

Bircas HaTorah / בִּרְכַּת הַתּוֹרָה

One of the first things we do every morning is thank Hashem for giving us His Torah and letting us learn it

Blessed are You, Hashem, our God, King of the universe, Who has made us holy with His mitzvos, and has commanded us to learn Torah. And please, Hashem, make the Torah pleasant to us, and to all of Your people. May we and our children understand You and study Your Torah simply because You told us to study it. Blessed are You, Hashem, Who teaches Torah to His nation, Israel.

בָּרוּךְ אַתָּה יהוה אֱלֹהֵינוּ מֶלֶךְ הָעוֹלָם, אֲשֶׁר קִדְּשָׁנוּ בְּמִצְוֹתָיו, וְצִוָּנוּ לַעֲסֹק בְּדִבְרֵי תוֹרָה. וְהַעֲרֶב נָא יהוה אֱלֹהֵינוּ אֶת דִּבְרֵי תוֹרָתְךָ בְּפִינוּ וּבְפִי עַמְּךָ בֵּית יִשְׂרָאֵל. וְנִהְיֶה אֲנַחְנוּ וְצֶאֱצָאֵינוּ וְצֶאֱצָאֵי עַמְּךָ בֵּית יִשְׂרָאֵל, כֻּלָּנוּ יוֹדְעֵי שְׁמֶךָ וְלוֹמְדֵי תוֹרָתֶךָ לִשְׁמָהּ. בָּרוּךְ אַתָּה יהוה, הַמְלַמֵּד תּוֹרָה לְעַמּוֹ יִשְׂרָאֵל.

Blessed are You, Hashem, our God, King of the universe, Who chose us from all the other nations, and gave us His Torah. Blessed are You, Hashem, Who gives the Torah.

בָּרוּךְ אַתָּה יהוה אֱלֹהֵינוּ מֶלֶךְ הָעוֹלָם, אֲשֶׁר בָּחַר בָּנוּ מִכָּל הָעַמִּים וְנָתַן לָנוּ אֶת תּוֹרָתוֹ. בָּרוּךְ אַתָּה יהוה, נוֹתֵן הַתּוֹרָה.

After making the berachah, we say these verses from the Torah.

May Hashem bless you, and watch over you. May the Light of Hashem shine upon you. May Hashem look favorably on you, and bring you peace.

יְבָרֶכְךָ יהוה וְיִשְׁמְרֶךָ. יָאֵר יהוה פָּנָיו אֵלֶיךָ וִיחֻנֶּךָּ. יִשָּׂא יהוה פָּנָיו אֵלֶיךָ, וְיָשֵׂם לְךָ שָׁלוֹם.

A Closer Look

Berachos are not only important for the person saying the *berachah* but also for the person listening. After you hear someone else say a *berachah*, you must answer *Amen*.

If you answer *Amen* to a *berachah*, you receive a mitzvah as if you were the one who said that *berachah*.

Did You Know??

Amen — אָמֵן — is an abbreviation for *Eil Melech Ne'eman* — Hashem, the King, can be trusted.

It can also have different meanings. Sometimes the word *Amen* אָמֵן means אֱמוּנָה (belief), which means, "Yes, I believe this is true." And sometimes it can mean, "I also hope that will happen."

Amen is like a signature on an important paper, showing that we agree to everything on the paper.

Tzitzis / צִיצָת

Boys take their tallis kattan and check to make sure the tzitzis are not torn. Then they say:

בָּרוּךְ אַתָּה יהוה אֱלֹהֵינוּ מֶלֶךְ הָעוֹלָם, אֲשֶׁר קִדְּשָׁנוּ בְּמִצְוֹתָיו, וְצִוָּנוּ עַל מִצְוַת צִיצָת.

Blessed are You, Hashem, our God, King of the universe, Who has made us holy with His mitzvos, and commanded us about the mitzvah of *tzitzis*.

Now you put on the tallis kattan. If someone wears a tallis during Shacharis, he does not say this berachah. He should have the tallis kattan in mind when he says the berachah on his tallis.

A Closer Look
Making a *berachah* connects our body (the physical world) to our soul (the spiritual world). It shows that even our physical world was given to us by Hashem.

Did You Know??
Most men start wearing a *tallis* for davening when they get married. Among many people whose families come from Sephardic countries or Germany, a *tallis* is worn even by young boys.

34

Mezuzah / מְזוּזָה

When you attach a mezuzah to a doorpost, you say:

בָּרוּךְ אַתָּה יהוה אֱלֹהֵינוּ מֶלֶךְ הָעוֹלָם, אֲשֶׁר קִדְּשָׁנוּ בְּמִצְוֹתָיו, וְצִוָּנוּ לִקְבֹּעַ מְזוּזָה.

Blessed are You, Hashem, our God, King of the universe, Who has made us holy with His mitzvos, and commanded us to attach a *mezuzah*.

A Closer Look

The *mezuzah* is a page of parchment that has the holy words of the first two paragraphs of the *Shema* written on it. The letters are written with special ink, by a scribe called a *sofer*. Every few years an expert must check to make sure that every letter is still intact, and there are no mistakes in even one of the words.

Did You Know??

We attach a *mezuzah* on an angle, leaning toward the inside of the house or the room. The reason it is at an angle is because one opinion says that we attach the *mezuzah* straight up, and another opinion says that we attach the *mezuzah* lying on its side. So we "compromise" and attach it on an angle. Sephardic Jews attach their *mezuzah* straight up.

Lulav and Esrog / נְטִילַת לוּלָב

Every morning of Succos, you take the lulav with your right hand (if you are right-handed), and then you take the esrog (with the pitum facing down) with your left hand. After you say the following berachos, you turn over the esrog and wave the lulav and esrog in six different directions. On Shabbos we do not take the lulav and esrog.

Blessed are You, Hashem, our God, King of the universe, Who has made us holy with His mitzvos, and commanded us about the taking of a *lulav* (palm branch).

בָּרוּךְ אַתָּה יהוה אֱלֹהֵינוּ מֶלֶךְ הָעוֹלָם, אֲשֶׁר קִדְּשָׁנוּ בְּמִצְוֹתָיו, וְצִוָּנוּ עַל נְטִילַת לוּלָב.

The next berachah, the Shehecheyanu (see page 41), is added only on the first day of Succos.

Blessed are You, Hashem, our God, King of the universe, for keeping us alive, taking care of us, and bringing us to this time.

בָּרוּךְ אַתָּה יהוה אֱלֹהֵינוּ מֶלֶךְ הָעוֹלָם, שֶׁהֶחֱיָנוּ וְקִיְּמָנוּ וְהִגִּיעָנוּ לַזְּמַן הַזֶּה.

A Closer Look

The *esrog*, *lulav*, *haddasim*, and *aravos* are called the *Arba'ah Minnim* (the *Four Species*). Each of them is shaped like a different part of the body. The *esrog* is shaped like the heart, the *lulav* is shaped like the spine, the *haddasim* are shaped like the eyes, and the *aravos* are shaped like the mouth. When we wave the *Arba'ah Minnim* together, we do this mitzvah with all our heart and all our body.

Did You Know??

The *esrog*, which both smells good and tastes good, is compared to a *tzaddik*. A *tzaddik* both studies Torah and does good deeds.

The *lulav* is the branch of a date tree. Dates taste good but have no special smell. This is compared to a person who studies Torah but does not do good deeds.

The *haddasim*, which smell good but have no taste, are compared to a person who does not study Torah but does good deeds.

The *aravos*, which have no smell and no taste, are compared to a person who doesn't study Torah and doesn't do good deeds.

We make the blessing and wave all four together to show that all Jews, no matter what. are all important.

Candle Lighting / הַדְלָקַת נֵרוֹת

Before Shabbos starts, we light the candles and say this berachah:

Blessed are You, Hashem, our God, King of the universe, Who has made us holy with His mitzvos, and commanded us to light the Shabbos lights.

בָּרוּךְ אַתָּה יהוה אֱלֹהֵינוּ מֶלֶךְ הָעוֹלָם, אֲשֶׁר קִדְּשָׁנוּ בְּמִצְוֹתָיו, וְצִוָּנוּ לְהַדְלִיק נֵר שֶׁל שַׁבָּת.

When we light the Yom Tov candles, we say this berachah:
(when Yom Tov comes out on Shabbos we add the the words in brackets):

Blessed are You, Hashem, our God, King of the universe, Who has made us holy with His mitzvos, and commanded us to light the [Shabbos lights and the] Yom Tov lights.

בָּרוּךְ אַתָּה יהוה אֱלֹהֵינוּ מֶלֶךְ הָעוֹלָם, אֲשֶׁר קִדְּשָׁנוּ בְּמִצְוֹתָיו, וְצִוָּנוּ לְהַדְלִיק נֵר שֶׁל [שַׁבָּת וְשֶׁל] יוֹם טוֹב.

On the first day of Yom Tov in Eretz Yisrael (outside Eretz Yisrael, on the first two days of Yom Tov), we also add the following berachah, the Shehecheyanu (see page 41):

Blessed are You, Hashem, our God, King of the universe, for keeping us alive, taking care of us, and bringing us to this time.

בָּרוּךְ אַתָּה יהוה אֱלֹהֵינוּ מֶלֶךְ הָעוֹלָם, שֶׁהֶחֱיָנוּ וְקִיְּמָנוּ וְהִגִּיעָנוּ לַזְּמַן הַזֶּה.

Did You Know??

Shabbos is a chance for us to be free from all the work of the week. We should feel close to Hashem and think about our connection to Him. Our Sages teach us that if all Jews would observe just two Shabbosos in a row, Mashiach would come.

Shemini Atzeres, which comes right after Succos, is really a new Yom Tov. We make a *Shehecheyanu* when lighting candles on Shemini Atzeres (and outside Eretz Yisrael, on Simchas Torah).

A Closer Look

When a woman lights the Shabbos candles, she welcomes the holy Shabbos. This is a time when a woman has a special connection to Hashem, and therefore it is a good time for her to pray for her family and for things that she needs.

Hashem created the world in six days and on the seventh day He rested. He filled the seventh day (Shabbos) with holiness. Since that first Shabbos, every seventh day has received this special holiness directly from Hashem. It is a day to be spent praying, singing at the Shabbos table, and learning with your family.

Chanukah Candles / נֵרוֹת חֲנֻכָּה

On the first night of Chanukah, we say the following three berachos.
On each of the next nights, only the first two berachos are said.

Blessed are You, Hashem, our God, King of the universe, Who has made us holy with His mitzvos, and commanded us to light the Chanukah light.

בָּרוּךְ אַתָּה יהוה אֱלֹהֵינוּ מֶלֶךְ הָעוֹלָם, אֲשֶׁר קִדְּשָׁנוּ בְּמִצְוֹתָיו, וְצִוָּנוּ לְהַדְלִיק נֵר (שֶׁל) חֲנֻכָּה.

Blessed are You, Hashem, our God, King of the universe, Who has made miracles for our fathers, in those days at this time of the year.

בָּרוּךְ אַתָּה יהוה אֱלֹהֵינוּ מֶלֶךְ הָעוֹלָם, שֶׁעָשָׂה נִסִּים לַאֲבוֹתֵינוּ, בַּיָּמִים הָהֵם בַּזְּמַן הַזֶּה.

The next berachah, the Shehecheyanu (see page 41), is added only on the first night of Chanukah.

Blessed are You, Hashem, our God, King of the universe, for keeping us alive, taking care of us, and bringing us to this time.

בָּרוּךְ אַתָּה יהוה אֱלֹהֵינוּ מֶלֶךְ הָעוֹלָם, שֶׁהֶחֱיָנוּ וְקִיְּמָנוּ וְהִגִּיעָנוּ לַזְּמַן הַזֶּה.

On the first night we light the candle on the far right of the menorah. On each of the following nights, a new candle is added and lit to the left of the candle of the night before. The new candle is lit first and we then light each candle to the right. On the eighth night, we light all eight candles.

A Closer Look

On Chanukah we celebrate the defeat of the Greek-Syrians by the Jewish people, led by the Chashmonaim. The first thing they did was go to the *Bais HaMikdash* and put up a Menorah — but they found only one jug of pure oil. It had enough oil to burn for only one night. A miracle happened and the oil burned for eight days. This is why we celebrate Chanukah for eight days.

The Chanukah lights are holy and therefore we are not allowed to use their light for any other purpose, such as reading.

The Chanukah candles must stay lit for at least 30 minutes after dark.

Did You Know??

On Chanukah people eat *latkes* (potato pancakes), and *sufganiyot* (fried jelly donuts). These foods are all fried in oil, and reminds us that the miracle of Chanukah happened with oil.

Do you know which *berachah* we make on *latkes*, and which *berachah* we make on fried jelly donuts?

See answer, upside down, at bottom of page.

Answer: On *latkes*, which are made out of potatoes, we say a *Borei Pri HaAdamah*. On jelly donuts we say *Borei Minei Mezonos*.

38

Section 3

בִּרְכַּת הַהוֹדָאָה וְהַשֶּׁבַח

Bircas HaHoda'ah V'HaShevach

Berachos on hearing and seeing things that happen.

Asher Yatzar / אֲשֶׁר יָצַר

After going to the bathroom, we say the following berachah:

בָּרוּךְ אַתָּה יהוה אֱלֹהֵינוּ מֶלֶךְ הָעוֹלָם, אֲשֶׁר יָצַר אֶת הָאָדָם בְּחָכְמָה, וּבָרָא בוֹ נְקָבִים נְקָבִים, חֲלוּלִים חֲלוּלִים. גָּלוּי וְיָדוּעַ לִפְנֵי כִסֵּא כְבוֹדֶךָ, שֶׁאִם יִפָּתֵחַ אֶחָד מֵהֶם, אוֹ יִסָּתֵם אֶחָד מֵהֶם, אִי אֶפְשַׁר לְהִתְקַיֵּם וְלַעֲמוֹד לְפָנֶיךָ. בָּרוּךְ אַתָּה יהוה, רוֹפֵא כָל בָּשָׂר וּמַפְלִיא לַעֲשׂוֹת.

Blessed are You, Hashem, our God, King of the universe, Who has made man with wisdom. You created man with a body that has many openings and parts. You know that if even one part of our body is blocked and does not work properly, it would be impossible for us to live. Blessed are You, Hashem, Who heals people and does wondrous things.

A Closer Look

Berachos remind us that the purpose of our lives is to make ourselves holy.

When we make a *berachah*, we are showing that we understand that Hashem created the world and continues to run it every day. Even though Hashem is so holy, He is still involved in making sure a person's physical body works properly. We know that Hashem is involved in *every* part of our lives.

Did You Know??

All *berachos* show *hakaros hatov* (gratitude). We say *thank You* to Hashem and show that we are grateful for the good that He does for us. Even after we go to the bathrooom, we thank Hashem for making our bodies work so well.

Shehecheyanu / שֶׁהֶחֱיָנוּ

When you eat a new fruit for the first time in the new season, or put on an important new item of clothing for the first time, or do a mitzvah that comes just once a year (like matzoh or succah), you say:

Blessed are You, Hashem, our God, King of the universe, for keeping us alive, taking care of us, and bringing us to this time.

בָּרוּךְ אַתָּה יהוה אֱלֹהֵינוּ מֶלֶךְ הָעוֹלָם, שֶׁהֶחֱיָנוּ וְקִיְּמָנוּ וְהִגִּיעָנוּ לַזְּמַן הַזֶּה.

Did You Know??
It is important to concentrate on what you are saying when you make a *berachah*, and to realize you are thanking Hashem with each *berachah* that you make.

You should not be doing anything else while you are making a *berachah*.

A Closer Look
When Hashem gives us something new and important, we thank Him for letting us live to enjoy it.

Lightning / בָּרָק

When you see lightning or other natural wonders, such as a shooting star, or, according to many opinions, Niagara Falls, the Grand Canyon, or the Swiss Alps, you say:

Blessed are You, Hashem, our God, King of the universe, Who makes the works of Creation.

בָּרוּךְ אַתָּה יהוה אֱלֹהֵינוּ מֶלֶךְ הָעוֹלָם, עֹשֶׂה מַעֲשֵׂה בְרֵאשִׁית.

A Closer Look

When you make a *berachah* you must have the proper *kavanah* (intention). You must know what you are saying and why you are saying it.

We sometimes get upset when it rains, because it may spoil our plans for that day. But the world needs rain. We pray for rain at the right time so the crops will grow and we will have enough drinking water. In Eretz Yisrael it does not rain at all for about six months every year, so everyone is very happy when it rains

Thunder / רַעַם

When you hear thunder, you say:

בָּרוּךְ אַתָּה יהוה אֱלֹהֵינוּ מֶלֶךְ הָעוֹלָם, שֶׁכֹּחוֹ וּגְבוּרָתוֹ מָלֵא עוֹלָם.

Blessed are You, Hashem, our God, King of the universe, Whose strength and power fill the entire universe.

A Closer Look
Each *berachah* has a simple meaning — the basic translation — but also, each *berachah* has deeper meanings. The loud sound of thunder reminds us of Hashem's great strength.

Did You Know??
When the Torah was given by Hashem to the Jewish people at Har Sinai, there was much thunder and lightning. The Torah says that the people were able to see not just the lightning, but even the thunder.

43

Rainbow / קֶשֶׁת

When you see a rainbow in the sky, you say:

בָּרוּךְ אַתָּה יהוה אֱלֹהֵינוּ מֶלֶךְ הָעוֹלָם, זוֹכֵר הַבְּרִית, וְנֶאֱמָן בִּבְרִיתוֹ, וְקַיָּם בְּמַאֲמָרוֹ.

Blessed are You, Hashem, our God, King of the universe, Who remembers the promise He made to Noach not to destroy the world again, and does what He says He will do.

A Closer Look

Over four thousand years ago, Hashem saw that the people in the world were behaving very badly. The only really good man was Noach. Hashem decided to destroy all the people in the world by bringing a flood. He commanded Noach to build a giant boat, and bring his family and at least two of all the animals of the world into the boat. We call it Noach's Ark. During the flood, the whole world was destroyed except for Noach, his family, and the animals that were in the ark. When the earth was dry again, Hashem promised Noach that He would never destroy the world again with a flood. The sign Hashem gave to Noach as a reminder of this promise was the rainbow.

Did You Know??

Hashem's promise is that there will not be another flood even if people are wicked. In some generations there were such great *tzaddikim* that no rainbow appeared.

Ocean / יָם

When you see the ocean, you say:

Blessed are You, Hashem, our God, King of the universe, Who made the Great Sea.

בָּרוּךְ אַתָּה יהוה אֱלֹהֵינוּ מֶלֶךְ הָעוֹלָם, שֶׁעָשָׂה אֶת הַיָּם הַגָּדוֹל.

Did You Know??
Even though the great natural wonders that Hashem created already have their own *berachah*, "Who makes the works of creation," (see page 42), our Rabbis teach us that the oceans (and according to some, the Mediterranean Sea, also) are so special that they have their own blessing.

Fruit Tree Blooming / בִּרְכַּת הָאִילָנוֹת

When you see a fruit tree begin to blossom, you say:

בָּרוּךְ אַתָּה יהוה אֱלֹהֵינוּ מֶלֶךְ הָעוֹלָם, שֶׁלֹּא חִסַּר בְּעוֹלָמוֹ דָּבָר, וּבָרָא בוֹ בְּרִיּוֹת טוֹבוֹת וְאִילָנוֹת טוֹבִים, לֵהָנוֹת בָּהֶם בְּנֵי אָדָם.

Blessed are You, Hashem, our God, King of the universe, Who created a universe that has everything, Who created in that universe good creatures and good trees, which give pleasure to man.

Did You Know??

This *berachah* is said only one time each year, in the Spring, usually in the month of *Nissan* (Pesach-time).

It is best to say this *berachah* when you see two trees blooming at the same time, but if there is only one tree, you can still say the *berachah*.

In the southern hemisphere, in places such as Australia and South Africa, trees blossom during the months of Elul and Tishrei. In those countries, that is when you should say the *berachah*.

בְּשׂוֹרוֹת טוֹבוֹת
Good News

When you hear very good news that benefits you and others, you say:

בָּרוּךְ אַתָּה יהוה אֱלֹהֵינוּ מֶלֶךְ הָעוֹלָם, הַטּוֹב וְהַמֵּטִיב.

Blessed are You, Hashem, our God, King of the universe, Who is good and does good.

Did You Know??
If the news is good only for you, and no one else is involved, you say the *berachah "Shehecheyanu"* (page 41).

בְּשׂוֹרוֹת רָעוֹת
Bad News

When a person hears very bad news, he says:

בָּרוּךְ אַתָּה יהוה אֱלֹהֵינוּ מֶלֶךְ הָעוֹלָם, דַּיַּן הָאֱמֶת.

Blessed are You, Hashem, our God, King of the universe, Who is the true Judge.

Did You Know??
We often think we know what is best for us. But in truth, only Hashem knows what is really best for us. That is why, even when we hear bad news, we bless Hashem, because we understand that even the bad news is really, in some way, for the good.

When we hear bad news, we should say, "This too is for the best."

Torah Scholar / חַכְמֵי יִשְׂרָאֵל

When you see one of the generation's greatest Torah scholars, you say:

בָּרוּךְ אַתָּה יהוה אֱלֹהֵינוּ מֶלֶךְ הָעוֹלָם, שֶׁחָלַק מֵחָכְמָתוֹ לִירֵאָיו.

Blessed are You, Hashem, our God, King of the universe, Who has shared some of His knowledge with those people who fear him.

A Closer Look
In the same way that we respect our parents, we must also respect a great Torah scholar who has learned Hashem's wisdom. Our parents brought us into this world. A *rav* who teaches us Torah and mitzvos brings us into the eternal World to Come.

Did You Know??
The Jewish people consider learning Torah more important than any possessions that anyone might have. The Torah Sage is the most important person in your community.